AT THE PIANO WITH
THE SONS OF BACH
Edited by MAURICE HINSON

MIT DEN BACH-SÖHNEN AM KLAVIER
Herausgegeben von MAURICE HINSON

AU PIANO AVEC LES FILS DE BACH
Édité par MAURICE HINSON

GW00480846

© Copyright MCMXC by Alfred Publishing Co., Inc.
This edition published in 2002 by Faber Music
in association with Alfred Publishing Co., Inc.
3 Queen Square London WC1N 3AU
Cover design by Nick Flower
Cover illustration by Ted Engelbart
Music processed by Jackie Leigh
Übersetzung Dorothee Göbel
Traduction Faber Music
Printed in England by Caligraving Ltd

ISBN 0-571-52173-8 / 418 UK

Published by Faber Music in association
with Alfred Publishing Co., Inc.
Distributed worldwide by Faber Music Limited

FABER ff MUSIC

CONTENTS

WILHELM FRIEDEMANN BACH
(1710–1784)

Air . . . . *page 4*
Allegro . . . . *page 6*
Minuet . . . . *page 8*
Polonaise . . . . *page 9*

CARL PHILIPP EMANUEL BACH
(1714–1788)

Affettuoso . . . . *page 10*
March in D . . . . *page 12*
Menuet . . . . *page 14*
Solfeggio . . . . *page 15*

JOHANN CHRISTOPH FRIEDRICH BACH
(1732–1795)

Menuet . . . . *page 18*
'Ah, vous dirai-je, Maman': Theme and first variation . . . . . *page 19*

JOHANN CHRISTIAN BACH
(1735–1782)

Tempo giusto . . . . *page 20*
Toccata . . . . *page 22*

FOREWORD

Twenty children resulted from Johann Sebastian Bach's marriages to Maria Barbara and, later, Anna Magdalena. Only ten survived infancy: of these, four of the sons became famous musicians, working in cities (frequently appended to their names) throughout Europe during the eighteenth century.

The stylistic transition from the late Baroque to Classical period was almost something of a Bach family affair. While Johann Sebastian Bach (1685–1750) defined and summed up the Baroque musical language, his innovative sons struck new musical paths that opened the way to the Classical and Romantic eras. Wilhelm Friedemann (1710–1784) 'Halle' combined the new rhapsodic and improvisatory expressive style (*Empfindsamer Stil*), which characterized much European music at this time, with elements of linear polyphony learned from his father. Carl Philipp Emanuel (1714–1788) 'Berlin' developed this theme in his treatise of 1753, the *Essay on the True Art of Playing Keyboard Instruments*, in which he urges musicians to 'Play from the soul, not like a trained bird'.

For Johann Christoph Friedrich (1732–1795) 'Buckerberg' and Johann Christian (1735–1782) 'London', the expressive elements of *Empfindsamkeit* and the decorative Rococo were modified by the elegant Classical or *Galant* style. The nine-year-old Mozart, deeply impressed by the lyricism and melodic contrast of Johann Christian's music, arranged three of his keyboard sonatas as concertos (Köchel 107) in 1765 and mourned his death as 'a sad day for the world of music'.

These four sons of Bach all, to a greater or lesser extent, influenced the course of musical history in their day; their compositions have qualities that give them an importance for our own time. *At the Piano with the Sons of Bach* is a celebration of these qualities.

Andrew Higgins 2002

VORWORT

Aus Johann Sebastian Bachs Ehen mit Maria Barbara und später Anna Magdalena Bach gingen insgesamt zwanzig Kinder hervor, von denen zehn im frühen Kindesalter starben. Vier seiner Söhne wurden berühmte Musiker, die während des 18. Jahrhunderts in ganz Europa tätig waren – häufig fügte man dem Eigennamen „Bach" den Ort ihres Wirkens bei.

Den stilistischen Übergang vom Spätbarock zur Klassik kann man fast als ein familieninternes Ereignis der Bachs bezeichnen. Während Johann Sebastian Bach (1685–1750) die Musiksprache des Barock umgrenzte und zusammenfasste, schlugen seine einer neuen Musiksprache zugewandten Söhne musikalische Pfade ein, die den Weg zur klassischen und romantischen Musik ebneten. Wilhelm Friedemann (1710–1784), der „Hallische Bach", verband den neuen „Empfindsamen Stil", der einen Großteil der Musik Europas zu dieser Zeit prägte, mit kontrapunktischen Elementen, wie er sie bei seinem Vater erlernt hatte. Carl Philipp Emanuel (1714–1788), der „Berliner Bach", führte dies in seinem 1753 erschienenen Lehrbuch „Versuch über die wahre Art das Clavier zu spielen" weiter aus und verlangte von einem guten Musiker: „Aus der Seele muß man spielen, und nicht wie ein abgerichteter Vogel."

Für Johann Christoph Friedrich (1732–1795), den „Bückeburger Bach", und Johann Christian (1735–1782), den „Londoner Bach", führten die ausdruckshaften Elemente des Empfindsamen Stils und die Stilmittel des musikalischen Rokoko weiter zum eleganten „klassischen" oder auch „galanten Stil". Der neunjährige Mozart, von Gesanglichkeit und melodischem Kontrast in Johann Christians Werken stark beeindruckt, bearbeitete 1765 drei Klaviersonaten des Londoner Bachs als Konzerte (KV 107). Den Tod von Johann Christian Bach bezeichnete er als „schade für die Musikalische Welt".

Die vier Bach-Söhne beeinflussten zu ihrer Zeit in unterschiedlichem Maße den Verlauf der Musikgeschichte. Ihre ausgezeichneten Kompositionen stehen auch heute für sich. Die vorliegende Ausgabe „Mit den Bach-Söhnen am Klavier" ist ein überzeugendes Beispiel dieser besonderen Qualitäten.

Andrew Higgins 2002

AVANT-PROPOS

Des vingt enfant nés des mariages successifs de Johann Sebastian Bach avec Maria Barbara, puis Anna Magdalena, seuls dix passèrent le cap de la petite enfance et quatre, des garçons, devinrent des musiciens célèbres, qui travaillèrent dans des villes européennes (souvent apposées à leurs noms) tout au long du XVIIIᵉ siècle.

La transition stylistique entre le baroque tardif et la période classique fut, en quelque sorte, l'affaire de la famille Bach. Alors que Johann Sebastian (1685–1750) définit et synthétisa le langage musical baroque, ses fils, novateurs, découvrirent de nouveaux chemins musicaux qui ouvrirent la voie aux ères classique et romantique. Wilhelm Friedemann (1710–1784) «Halle» combina ainsi le nouveau style expressif rhapsodique, de caractère improvisé (*Empfindersamer Stil*), typique d'une grande partie de la musique européenne d'alors, à des éléments de polyphonie linéaire appris auprès de son père. Carl Philipp Emanuel (1714–1788) «Berlin» développa d'ailleurs ce thème dans son *Essai sur la véritable manière de jouer des instruments à clavier* (1753), traité dans lequel il exhorte les musiciens à «jouer avec leur âme, non comme des oiseaux savants».

Johann Christoph Friedrich (1732–1795) «Buckerberg» et Johann Christian (1735–1782) «Londres» virent, quant à eux, les éléments expressifs de l'*Empfindsamkeit* et le rococo décoratif modifiés par le style élégant classique ou galant. En 1765, profondément impressionné par le lyrisme et le contraste mélodique de la musique de Johann Christian, Mozart, alors âgé de neuf ans, arrangea sous forme de concertos (Köchel 107) trois de ses sonates pour clavier – et il pleura la mort de Johann Christian comme «une triste journée pour le monde de la musique».

Ces quatre fils de Bach influèrent tous, plus ou moins, sur le cours de l'histoire musicale de leur temps, et leurs compositions recèlent de telles qualités qu'elles n'ont en rien perdu de leur importance. Au piano avec les fils de Bach se veut la célébration de ces qualités.

Andrew Higgins 2002

AIR

Allegretto (♩ = *c.*72)

Wilhelm Friedemann Bach

ALLEGRO

Wilhelm Friedemann Bach

MINUET

Wilhelm Friedemann Bach

POLONAISE
NO. 4

Wilhelm Friedemann Bach

AFFETTUOSO

Carl Philipp Emanuel Bach

MARCH IN D

Carl Philipp Emanuel Bach
BWV Anh. 122

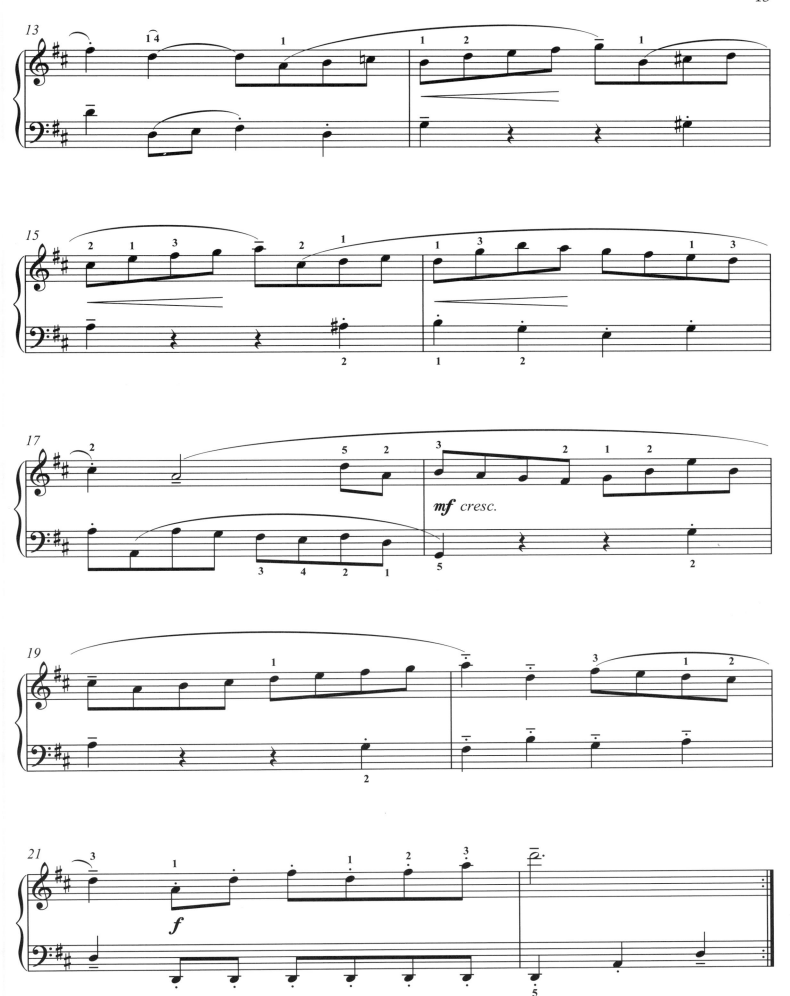

MENUET

Carl Philipp Emanuel Bach

SOLFEGGIO †

Carl Philipp Emanuel Bach
Wq. 117/2

† A *solfeggio* is properly a vocal study and rarely used with instrumental music.

Ein „Solfeggio" ist eigentlich eine Übung für die Stimme und findet sich selten als Bezeichnung instrumentaler Musik.

Un «solfeggio» étant, à proprement parler, une étude vocale, il est rarement utilisé avec de la musique instrumentale.

MENUET

Johann Christoph Friedrich Bach

'AH, VOUS DIRAI-JE, MAMAN'
THEME AND FIRST VARIATION

Johann Christoph Friedrich Bach

VARIATION 1

TEMPO GIUSTO

Johann Christian Bach

(b) Play on the beat as an acciaccatura.

Auf den Schlag wie einen Vorschlag spielen.

Jouez comme pour une acciaccatura.

TOCCATA

Johann Christian Bach